PUFFIN BOOKS

MR MAJEIKA AND THE SCHOOL PLAY

Humphrey Carpenter was born and educated in Oxford and worked for the BBC before becoming a full-time writer in 1975. He has published award-winning biographies of J. R. R. Tolkien, C. S. Lewis, W. H. Auden, Benjamin Britten, Spike Milligan and others, and is the co-author, with his wife, Mari Prichard, of *The Oxford Companion to Children's Literature*. From 1994 to 1996 he directed the Cheltenham Festival of Literature. He has written plays for radio and the theatre, including a dramatization of *Gulliver's Travels* (1995), and for many years ran a young people's drama group, the Mushy Pea Theatre Company. He has two daughters.

HUMPHREY CARPENTER

Mr Majeika and the School Play

Illustrated by Frank Rodgers

PUFFIN

PUFFIN BOOKS

Published by the Penguin Group
Penguin Books Ltd, 80 Strand, London WC2R 0RL, England
Penguin Group (USA) Inc., 375 Hudson Street, New York, New York 10014, USA
Penguin Books Australia Ltd, 250 Camberwell Road, Camberwell,
Victoria 3124, Australia
Penguin Books Canada Ltd, 10 Alcorn Avenue, Toronto, Ontario, Canada M4V 3B2
Penguin Books India (P) Ltd, 11 Community Centre, Panchsheel Park,
New Delhi – 110 017, India
Penguin Books (NZ) Ltd, Cnr Rosedale and Airborne Roads, Albany, Auckland,
New Zealand
Penguin Books (South Africa) (Pty) Ltd, 24 Sturdee Avenue, Rosebank 2196, South Africa

Penguin Books Ltd, Registered Offices: 80 Strand, London WC2R 0RL, England

www.penguin.com

First published by Viking 1991
Published in Puffin Books 1992
002

Text copyright © Humphrey Carpenter, 1991
Illustrations copyright © Frank Rodgers, 1991
All rights reserved

The moral right of the author and illustrator has been asserted

Set in Palatino

Made and printed in England by Clays Ltd, St Ives plc

British Library Cataloguing in Publication Data
A CIP catalogue record for this book is available from the British Library

ISBN-13: 978-0-141-34706-6

www.greenpenguin.co.uk

Penguin Books is committed to a sustainable
future for our business, our readers and our planet.
This book is made from Forest Stewardship
Council™ certified paper.

Contents

1. *Hamish and the People Next Door*

"As you all know," said Mr Majeika to Class Three at St Barty's School, "this term our project is mountains. And this morning we're going to watch a video called *The Conquest of Everest*."

Everyone in Class Three was pleased about this, except Hamish Bigmore, the worst-behaved boy in the class. "What a bore," he said, yawning.

"Why does Hamish always have to grumble?" said Pete to his twin brother Thomas. Their friend Jody said to Hamish: "It's a really exciting film. I've seen it before. It's about some very brave people who were the first to climb up Mount Everest, the highest mountain in the world."

1

"*Climb*," sneered Hamish. "What a silly thing to do. They ought to have got a plane to land them on the top."

Mr Majeika sighed. Teaching Class Three would have been very easy if it hadn't been for Hamish. Every time the class did anything unusual, Hamish complained and made a nuisance of himself. Then Mr Majeika would lose his temper and do some magic in order to set things right again.

Mr Majeika had once been a wizard, but he was now a teacher, and teachers aren't supposed to do magic. And if it hadn't been for Hamish Bigmore, Mr Majeika wouldn't have had to do any magic, and there would have been peace and quiet.

"Settle down, everyone," Mr Majeika called, and he switched on the television and the video recorder. The film began with some stirring music, and the words

"The Conquest of Everest" came up on the screen. Soon Class Three were watching the team of brave people climbing up through the snow towards the peak of the mountain.

Suddenly the picture stopped, and then the mountaineers began walking backwards. One or two people giggled, and Mr Majeika looked puzzled. "What's going on?" he asked. Although he knew lots about magic, he wasn't very good at coping with modern machines like televisions and video recorders, so he didn't realize what had happened.

"It's Hamish Bigmore, sir," called out Melanie. "He's got the remote control and he's mucking about with it." Hamish kicked Melanie and she began to cry.

"Stop it, Hamish," said Mr Majeika. The film went on normally for a few minutes. Then, just as the mountaineers were walking through a snowstorm, the picture changed into a Bugs Bunny cartoon.

"Hamish, what are you doing?" snapped Mr Majeika. "Give me that thing!" But Hamish had hidden the remote control in his desk, and Mr Majeika couldn't find it.

Once again, the Everest film continued for a couple of minutes. But just as it was getting really exciting, it all went into double speed, so that the mountaineers were running up Everest like Olympic sprinters. "There!" Hamish called out. "Climbing mountains is easy!"

"Hamish Bigmore, I have had *enough*," exploded Mr Majeika. There was a flash and a puff of smoke, and Hamish was nowhere to be seen.

"Hurray," said Jody. "Now we can watch the film in peace."

"Yes," said Thomas. "But what's

happened to Hamish?"

"I've no idea," said Mr Majeika, looking worried. "Silly me, I've been and done it again."

"There are no frogs around, sir," said one of the other children. On a famous occasion when Mr Majeika had first come to teach Class Three, he had accidentally turned Hamish into a frog, and it had taken a lot of bother to turn him back again.

"He'll turn up sooner or later, worse luck," said Pete. Mr Majeika thought this was probably true, so they all got on with watching the rest of the film, which was very exciting.

The only odd thing was that just after Hamish disappeared, the television set began rocking from side to side, as if someone were stuck in there and was trying to get out. Mr Majeika peered into the back of it, but he couldn't see anything unusual.

By the end of afternoon school, Hamish still hadn't turned up, and Mr Majeika was looking very anxious. "Oh dear," he muttered, "whatever will his parents say?"

"Don't worry, Mr Majeika," said Thomas. "They're away, and Hamish is staying with us, worse luck."

"We'll tell our mum he's staying with someone else tonight," said Pete. "I'm sure she'll be glad not to have him in the house."

"Well, I'll have to try out some spells tonight to see if I can find where he is," said Mr Majeika. "It's really very worrying." He went home and spent the evening turning the pages of his spell book. He tried out all sorts of spells for finding missing people, but without any success.

Meanwhile Jody had gone home and switched on the TV. When the children's programmes were finished, *The People Next Door* came on.

Most of Class Three, especially the girls, watched *The People Next Door*. It was an Australian programme about several families who lived in the same street. The characters everybody liked best were a young woman called Jolene and a young man called Craig, who were played by two famous pop stars. Jolene and Craig had fallen in love, and most evenings there were scenes of them kissing each other.

Thomas liked watching *The People Next Door*, and he tried to do his hair like Craig and speak with an Australian accent. Pete thought the programme was silly, though, and he usually went and did something else while it was on.

Jody had just poured herself a glass of orange juice and was watching the first scene of tonight's episode. Sure enough, there were Craig and Jolene sitting on a bench at the end of the street, in the moonlight.

"Oh, Craig," said Jolene.

"Oh, Jolene," said Craig.

"Oi," said a voice, "how do I get out of this crummy place and back to St Barty's?"

Jody froze. She knew that voice. It was Hamish Bigmore.

"Who was that, Craig?" whispered Jolene. "I thought we were all alone."

Craig looked around him. "Sure are," he said. "Can't see anyone. Just some kid in a back garden, I reckon . . . Oh, Jolene!"

"Oh, Craig!"

"Oi," said the voice again, "did you hear me? I said, how do I get out of this crummy place and back to St Barty's School?"

"There it is again, Craig," said Jolene.

"Well, I still can't see anyone," said

Craig. "Oh, Jolene!"

"Oh, Craig!" said Jolene.

They began to kiss.

But before they could get into a clinch, Hamish Bigmore's head came up over the back of the bench. "Oi!" he said. "No snogging here!"

"Pete!" called Thomas, who was watching the programme in the living-room. "Come here! Hamish has got into *The People Next Door*!"

"And who do you think you are?" Jolene was saying angrily to Hamish.

"I've never seen him before," said Craig. "Are you from this street, kid?"

"Course I'm not from your crummy street," said Hamish. "This programme's a load of rubbish, everyone knows that. They ought to take it off and put on a horror movie. And as for you two, snogging all the time –"

"Get out of here," snapped Craig, raising his fists to Hamish.

"Sure, I'm going," sneered Hamish. He turned to Jolene. "I'm off to somewhere better than this. Fancy an evening out with me, honeybunch?"

"Why, you little twerp!" snapped Jolene, as Hamish ran off.

"Good grief," said Pete, staring at the TV set, "how did he get into the programme?"

The telephone rang. It was Jody. "Did you see what I saw?" she asked Thomas.

"Yes," said Thomas. "Just like him, barging in on Craig and Jolene."

"It must have been Mr Majeika's spell this morning," said Jody. "Let's keep watching, in case he comes back."

But the rest of *The People Next Door* went on without interruption.

Thomas and Pete had their supper and went to bed. But Thomas decided that he wanted a glass of water before he went to sleep. He went downstairs again.

In the living-room the TV was on, but no one was watching it. His father was in the kitchen, washing up, and his mother was writing a letter.

On the TV a famous newsreader was questioning the Prime Minister about new laws that had been passed for schools. "And does this mean, Prime Minister, that all children will have to do at least an hour's maths every day?"

"It certainly does," answered the Prime Minister. "We believe that maths is a very important subject. This country needs people who are good at maths, because –"

"What a load of rubbish," said Hamish's voice suddenly, and, as Thomas watched, Hamish himself appeared on the screen, just behind the Prime Minister's chair.

The Prime Minister stared. "Who is this impertinent young man?" she asked.

"Hamish Bigmore, Class Three, St Barty's School," said Hamish. "And you can take it from me that maths is the stupidest subject ever invented. What's the point of learning maths? You can do it all with calculators and computers. Anyway, I'm off."

"I'm terribly sorry about that, Prime Minister, and, er, viewers," said the

13

famous newsreader. "A slight technical hitch. Well, as you were saying, Prime Minister . . ." And the programme continued normally.

Thomas got his glass of water and went upstairs. "I've seen him again," he said to Pete. "He seems to be wandering through all the programmes."

"Well, I hope he stays there," said Pete, and he rolled over and went to sleep.

But Thomas couldn't get to sleep for thinking about Hamish, and wondering what programme he would turn up in next.

After about an hour, he got up and went downstairs again. His parents had gone to bed now, because it was very late. Thomas turned on the TV. A horror film was showing.

He looked in the paper. The film was called *The Curse of the Locked Room*, and it was about a family living in a haunted house where one of the rooms was locked. The film got spookier and spookier, and the music became creepier and creepier. At last it got to the scene where they had found the key to the locked room, and were going to open it.

It was a very old film, in black and white.

"Oh, Claude," said the heroine, "do you think it's safe for us to – to open that mysterious door?"

"We must do, my darling," said the hero. "We can't go on living with this terrible menace in our lives. We have to find out what's – *in that room!*"

The two of them walked down the passage to the locked room, holding on to each other nervously. The hero put the key in the lock and turned it. "And now," he breathed, "we will see!"

He turned the handle and the door
creaked open.

"Oi," said Hamish's voice, "get out of
here. It's the middle of the night, and I'm
trying to get a bit of sleep."

The hero banged the door shut.
"Aaargh!" he gasped. "It was ghastly!
Let's leave it in there, my darling, and lock
the door again. If we let it out, who knows
what harm such a terrible creature might do?'

"That's true enough," said Thomas to himself, and went to bed.

The next morning at school, Mr Majeika was looking very anxious indeed. "Has anyone seen Hamish Bigmore?" he asked nervously. "I can't discover him anywhere."

"I saw him, Mr Majeika," said Jody. "He was standing behind a bench in Australia."

"And Thomas saw him talking to the Prime Minister," said Pete.

"And he was in a locked room in a haunted house," said Thomas.

"This is no time for silly games," said Mr Majeika.

"No, really," said Thomas, and he and Jody explained.

Mr Majeika turned rather white and looked very concerned. "This is terrible," he said. "How on earth are we to get him out? His parents will be horrified if they find out."

"And just think of the poor people whose TV programmes he keeps spoiling," said Jody.

"Very well," said Mr Majeika, "I'll see what I can do."

He thought for a moment, then shut his eyes and waved his hands over the television set. Nothing happened.

"Oh dear," he said.

"Perhaps it would work if you turned the TV on?" suggested Jody.

"What a good idea," said Mr Majeika. He switched it on. "And now," the announcer was saying, "here's a Bugs Bunny cartoon."

The cartoon started. Mr Majeika shut his eyes and waved his hands again.

Bugs Bunny came running on to the screen – and came running off the screen, right out into the classroom.

"Hi there!" he said to Mr Majeika. "What's up, doc?"

Mr Majeika hastily waved his hands again, and Bugs Bunny disappeared back on to the screen.

"You should have left him here, Mr Majeika," said Pete. "He could have had Hamish Bigmore's desk. I'd much rather sit next to Bugs Bunny than Hamish Bigmore."

The cartoon came to an end and a programme for very young children began. "Hello, everyone," said the jolly lady who was presenting it. "Today I'm going to show you what to make with Play-doh. Now, here's something I made earlier . . ."

Hamish Bigmore walked across the screen, yawning. "I want some breakfast," he said to the lady presenter. "Hasn't anyone got anything to eat in this dump?" He walked off again, in search of food.

"This is dreadful," said Mr Majeika. "What am I going to do?"

"Next time he comes on the screen," said Jody, "you could try your spell again. After all, it brought Bugs Bunny out, so why not Hamish?"

But Hamish didn't reappear in the children's programme, so they had to wait to see what would come on next.

It was a Western, with lots of cowboys. For a long while, there was no sign of Hamish. Then the scene switched to a saloon, and while the two main characters were drinking at the bar, the doors swung open and in walked Hamish.

He was dressed as a cowboy, with a big hat and pistols slung on each side. "Good grief," said Thomas. "Where on earth did he get those clothes?"

"Howdy, pardner," said one of the cowboys.

"Howdy," said Hamish.

"What are you having, Big Boy?" said
the blonde barmaid.

"I'll have cornflakes and baked beans on
toast," said Hamish. "And what are you
doing tonight, sweetheart?"

"Hey, pardner," said the other cowboy,
"you lay off mah gal!" And he put his
hands on his pistols.

"Want a fight, do you?" said Hamish,

taking out both of his pistols, pointing them in the cowboy's face and pulling the triggers.

They were water-pistols, and water squirted all over the cowboy's face.

"Aaargh!" roared the cowboy. "I'm gonna get you for that. This town ain't big enough for both of us."

Hamish leapt over the bar tables and ran out through the door. The big cowboy was after him, but Hamish tore off down the main street.

Mr Majeika shut his eyes and waved his hands, and Hamish ran out of the television screen and into Class Three.

He collapsed, very out of breath, into his own chair at his own desk.

"Well," said Jody, "did you have a good time?"

Hamish was still wearing his cowboy outfit. "It was better than being in this

crummy school," he said.

On the screen, the big cowboy was still searching for Hamish. After a while he gave up and went back to finish his drink at the bar.

"It won't be much of a film without *me* in it," said Hamish. "I was in *The People Next Door*, did you know that? And Jolene fancied me much more than Craig."

"What rubbish," said Jody. "She couldn't stand you."

"Now that Hamish is back," said Mr Majeika, "let's get on with our project. And Hamish, if I have any more trouble from you, I'll send you back inside the TV. This time I'll make sure you land up in the Everest film and have to climb to the top. So behave yourself!"

Hamish twirled his pistols and muttered, but got on quietly with his project.

When he handed it in a few days later, he had written on the front:

This project is by
HAMISH BIGMORE
Star of *The People Next Door*
and many other TV shows.
Signed photos for sale.

"I suppose the next thing," said Jody, "he'll be starting a Hamish Bigmore Fan Club."

"Still, I must say, the TV programmes are rather boring without him," said Thomas.

2. *Hamish the Giant-Killer*

"This term," announced Mr Potter, the head teacher of St Barty's, at assembly one morning, "we shall be doing another school play. And we won't just be performing it here, to the parents. St Barty's is entering for the County Schools' Drama Cup. We shall be taking our play to a big drama festival at another school, where all the entries will be judged by a Famous Actor. The cast of the winning play will receive the Cup. Let's hope St Barty's wins!"

Most of the school were pleased at the news, but everyone in Class Three groaned. The trouble with school plays was Hamish Bigmore. Somehow or other, he always managed to ruin them.

When Hamish had first come to St Barty's, Mr Potter had given him a very small part in a nativity play. He was supposed to be an ox at the stable in Bethlehem. The trouble was, as soon as anyone else started talking, he began making loud mooing noises, so that it was impossible for the play to continue.

Mr Potter decided that if Hamish had a big part, he might behave himself better. The next school play was a musical about Oliver Twist, and Hamish was given the part of the Artful Dodger.

The Artful Dodger is someone who goes around picking people's pockets – stealing their money and things, when they're not looking. Hamish took the part very seriously. As well as picking people's pockets on stage, he went and picked the audience's pockets during the interval, and they weren't very pleased when they

found that all their money and other things had gone.

After that, Mr Potter refused to give him a part in the next play. But he managed to ruin it all the same.

It was a very serious and sad play, and Jody took the part of a princess who was dying of a broken heart. Just as she began her dying speech, Hamish marched into the back of the hall with a tray slung round his neck, shouting: ''Ice-creams! Popcorn!

Drinks! Crisps!"

When Mr Majeika told Class Three that the play St Barty's would be entering for the Schools' Drama Cup was *Jack and the Beanstalk*, Thomas and Pete groaned. "I suppose that means Hamish will want to be the Giant," said Pete.

But he didn't. He decided he wanted to be Jack. And to everyone's surprise, Mr Potter chose him for the part.

"Mr Potter says it's because he's got a loud voice," said Jody.

"That's true enough," said Thomas. "But it's very unfair on everyone else. He's bound to ruin the play."

"You can't complain," said Jody. "You're playing the Giant."

"I'm only playing half the Giant," said Thomas. "The bottom half."

"I'm the top," said Pete, who was going to sit on Thomas's shoulders.

"And he's very heavy," said Thomas.

The rehearsals went very well at first, because Hamish was away with flu and Mr Majeika read his part. Thomas and Pete's mum had made a very good costume for them to wear as the Giant. There was a huge head made out of papier mâché, with eyeholes for Pete to look out. Thomas, as the bottom half, wore a gigantic pair of

trousers and some enormous boots. They had some difficulty seeing where they were going, but once they'd got on stage, the Giant looked fine.

"Just like the real thing," said Mr Majeika.

"Do you mean you've seen a real giant, Mr Majeika?" asked Jody, who was playing Jack's mother.

"Not often," said Mr Majeika. "But there are one or two lurking about, if you know where to look for them."

"And are they like the Giant in *Jack and the Beanstalk*, Mr Majeika?" asked Thomas.

Mr Majeika nodded. "Rather nastier, if anything, Thomas. They'd certainly eat you up for dinner if they felt like it. If you ever stumble across one, take care!"

Jody shivered. "Well, it's a good thing we're not likely to meet one, Mr Majeika," she said.

When Hamish came back to school, he was surprisingly well behaved in rehearsals. "Perhaps he's still feeling poorly from the flu," said Pete. "It's not like him to be as sensible as this."

Mr Potter was very pleased with the way *Jack and the Beanstalk* was going. "I think we stand a very good chance of winning the Drama Cup," he said.

A few days later, Jody said to Pete and

Thomas: "I think Hamish Bigmore is up to something."

"Nothing new about that," said Pete. "What is it this time?"

"Well, you know St James's, that snooty school down the road? I've seen a couple of boys from there talking to Hamish in the street."

"So what?" said Thomas. "I can't think why anyone should want to talk to Hamish, but there's no law against it, is there?"

"Of course not, silly," said Jody. "But can't you guess what it might mean?"

"They could just have been friends of his," said Pete.

"Hamish hasn't got any friends," said Jody. "And St James's are taking part in the Drama Cup. Now do you see what I'm getting at?"

"But why should St James's want

Hamish Bigmore in their play?" asked Thomas.

"They don't, you ass," said Pete. "Jody thinks Hamish Bigmore is being bribed by St James's to muck up *our* play, so that they win."

"I don't know it for certain," said Jody, "but Hamish has certainly been eating an awful lot of chocolate lately, even more than usual. I wonder where it's been coming from. We'd better just watch out, that's all."

Jody told Mr Majeika what she thought might be going on, but Mr Majeika said he couldn't do anything about it. "And I'm sure Hamish wouldn't really want another school to win, would he?" he said.

Jody shook her head. "I just wouldn't trust Hamish at all," she said.

On the day of the Drama Cup, they all went by bus to the school where the

competition was being held. "Welcome, everyone," said the person who was organizing the competition. "There's a notice telling you where your dressing-rooms are. When you're ready, please come and sit in the hall to watch the other plays. And besides the Cup, the winning school will have a special tea, with lots of chocolate cake!"

When they had got their costumes ready, they all went and sat in the hall.

The Famous Actor who was going to judge the plays was taking his seat.

"I've seen him on TV," said Thomas. "He looks rather bored at having to sit through a lot of school plays."

The lights were turned off and the first play began. It was being performed by a school called St Philips, and it was a musical version of *The Pied Piper*. It went on for a very long time, and Jody, Thomas and Pete could see that the Famous Actor was getting very bored. He kept yawning and looking at his watch.

When St Philips had finished there was a pause, and then St James's began their play. They were doing a detective story, and it was very exciting. People kept getting murdered, and there were lots of bangs and screams, which made the audience jump. Melanie started to cry.

When it was over everyone clapped a lot, and the Famous Actor looked as if he had enjoyed it.

"We've got to do really well to beat that," said Jody, as they hurried off to their dressing-room to get changed. "Let's hope Hamish doesn't let us down."

Hamish was being as good as gold as he climbed into his costume, but there was a naughty glint in his eye.

"Good luck, everyone," said Mr Majeika. "I'll be out at the front, watching you."

They all took their positions on stage.

The curtains opened and the first scene began.

At first, everything went smoothly. Jody was very good as Jack's mother, and Hamish spoke his lines clearly as Jack. The only mishap was in the scene where Jack

takes the cow to market and sells it for a handful of beans. Melanie was playing the front half of the cow and Pandora Green the back half. Pandora accidentally bumped rather hard into Melanie, and Melanie started crying. But she cried so loudly that it sounded like "Moo!", and the audience seemed to think it was part of the play.

While this scene was going on, Thomas and Pete climbed into the Giant's costume. "Wait a minute," said Pete. "Something funny is going on here. I can't find the eyeholes in the Giant's head."

"Let's have a look," said Thomas. "No wonder you can't – someone's blocked them up with glue and paper."

"Guess who," said Pete angrily. "I'll get him when the play's over. But I'll have to make new holes." He found a pencil and bored new holes for the eyes.

"Hurry up," said Thomas. "We're on in a moment."

Pete put on the Giant's head. "Bother," he said, "the holes are in the wrong place.

I can't see out of them at all. You'll have to steer us."

"But I can't see out either," said Thomas. "There was a little window in the costume for me to look through, but it's been covered over with black paint. We'll just have to feel our way on stage."

Just at that moment, Hamish Bigmore spoke the line that was Thomas and Pete's cue for going on. "But hark! What is this I hear? Can it be the Giant?"

"Quick!" hissed Thomas. "Say the line!"

Pete was supposed to boom out: "Fee, fie, fo, fum, I smell the blood of an Englishman", as the two of them walked on to the stage.

"Fee, fie, fo," he began, and then "Ouch!" because he and Thomas had walked into a piece of scenery.

Thomas and Pete couldn't see anything, but they could hear the audience roaring

with laughter. "This is terrible," hissed
Thomas. "Say it again."

"Fee, fie, fo, fum," Pete began again, "I
smell the blood of an – Oooo! Help, watch
out, I'm falling!"

Thomas had gone too far down stage,
missed his footing, and almost fallen into
the audience. Pete lost his balance and
slipped to the ground, tearing the Giant's
costume as he landed. There they both lay,
in a heap, while the audience roared with
laughter.

"It's all your fault," Jody hissed at Hamish Bigmore from the wings. "You dirty, rotten traitor, what did they pay you for mucking up our play?"

In answer, Hamish reached behind a piece of scenery and brought out a large box of chocolates, which he waved at Jody. "A present from St James's," he whispered. "Someone had better shut the curtains, the St Barty's play has had it!"

Sure enough, the Famous Actor had got to his feet and was saying: "I think we'd better stop this play, as there seems to have been a bit of an accident. Let's go on to the next one, shall we?"

Jody peered round the wings into the audience. She could see Mr Majeika sitting in the front row. "Can't you do something?" she mouthed at him.

Mr Majeika nodded and waved his hands. Suddenly everything went very dark, and there was the sound of thunder. "Is this the next play?" called out the Famous Actor. "Or are they trying to go on with *Jack and the Beanstalk?*"

In a moment, he had his answer. For a distant voice was calling out the very words that Pete had been trying to say – not someone pretending to be huge and terrifying, but this time (Thomas and Pete could tell) someone who really *was*: "*Fee,*

fie, fo, fum, I smell the blood of an Englishman. Be he alive or be he dead, I'll grind his bones to make my bread." There was the sound of huge feet coming near.

"That's better," called out the Famous Actor. "I'm glad that, er," he looked at his sheet of paper, "St Barty's School has sorted itself out. Carry on, St Barty's."

At that moment, the doors into the hall crashed open and there stood a Giant – a

real one. He had a shaggy beard, and he was carrying a huge, stone club the size of a small motor car. *"Where is he?"* he roared out. *"Where's that Englishman whose blood I can smell?"*

"Good costume," said the Famous Actor, making a note on his piece of paper. "And good staging. I like the way you've brought this person in through the audience, St Barty's. And the make-up is excellent."

"There he is!" roared out the Giant, spotting the Famous Actor. *"That's the fellow! He'll make a tasty morsel in my Man Soup tonight. Ha, ha, little fellow, you're coming in my pocket!"*

The rest of the audience had realized that this wasn't any actor, but the real thing. There was panic and people began to scream as they made their way to the doors. The Giant gave them a glance, but it was the Famous Actor who had taken his fancy, and he began to stride across the hall towards him.

Jody ran down from the stage into the audience. "Help, Mr Majeika!" she panted. "You've overdone it a bit. Nobody's going to get a prize if the Famous Actor is put into the Giant's soup!"

Mr Majeika sighed. "I know," he said. "That's the trouble with these Giants, they're such headstrong, tiresome fellows. Now, if a fairy had been what was needed, we'd have had no trouble. But it was all I could think of."

The Giant had picked up the Famous Actor and was carrying him by the scruff of the neck towards the stage. Strangely, the Famous Actor still hadn't realized that it wasn't just a play. "Very good," he kept saying. "Most remarkable for a school play. This is really professional. And I like

the way you've involved members of the
audience. Very good stuff."

The Giant reached the edge of the stage
and sat down on it, still holding on to the
Famous Actor. *"I know what I'm going to
do,"* he roared. *"I'm not going to wait to put
you in my Man Soup. I'm going to make a Man
Snack out of you right now. Nothing like fresh
Man when you're feeling peckish."* And he
opened his mouth and prepared to pop the

Famous Actor into it.

Then he saw Hamish Bigmore's box of chocolates.

"Whassat?" he cried. *"Is that chockies? I LOVE chockies. Gimme!"* And he reached out for them.

"Oi!" rang out a voice. "Hands off!" It was Hamish Bigmore. No one was going to steal his chocolates and get away with it, not even a man-eating Giant.

"*And 'oo are YOU?*" roared the Giant.

"I," said Hamish Bigmore, stepping forward and raising his sword (which was made of cardboard), "I am Jack the Giant-Killer. You've heard of me, haven't you?"

"*Y–yes,*" said the Giant, "*I h–have. Sorry, Mr Jack, sir. Blimey, I'm off!*" And taking to his heels, he ran through the doors and out of the hall, leaving the Famous Actor lying on the stage.

"Is that the end?" said the Famous Actor rather breathlessly. "Well done, everyone in St Barty's. Give them all a big round of applause."

And everyone went back to their seats and clapped, supposing that it must have been part of the play after all, and not a real Giant.

There was one more play after this, a scene from Shakespeare, but after all the business with the Giant, it seemed terribly dull. When it was over, the Famous Actor went up on to the stage.

"Well, you've all done splendidly," he said, "but I have no difficulty in deciding the winner. It's St Barty's!"

Everyone from St Barty's cheered and gathered round Mr Majeika, who had been given the Schools' Drama Cup. "Thank you, Mr Majeika," said Jody. "But it was a near thing, wasn't it?"

"Yes," said Mr Majeika, wiping his brow. "It certainly was."

"I hate to say this," said Thomas, "but I think Hamish Bigmore was rather brave."

"Not brave," said Pete, "just greedy. He'd do anything not to lose a box of chocolates."

"Who'd have known the Giant would be so frightened of Jack the Giant-Killer?" said Jody.

"All the Giants are," said Mr Majeika. "Are you surprised? In the story, he manages to kill three or four of them just like that."

"Talking of Jack the Giant-Killer," said Thomas. "Where is he?"

Mr Majeika looked around him. "He seems to have vanished. Perhaps he's gone after the Giant, though I'd have thought that Hamish's cardboard sword wouldn't be much use against a real Giant."

"Never mind," said Pete. "Who wants to waste time looking for Hamish Bigmore? Let's go and have that prize tea we were promised."

But when they got to the room where the tea was set out, there was just a mess of empty plates, with Hamish Bigmore sitting in the middle of them, looking rather sick.

"Guess what's happened to the

chocolate cake?" said Jody.

"Oh, Hamish," said Mr Majeika, "you might have left *some* for the rest of us."

"Fee, fie, fo, fum!" chanted Pete. "I smell the blood of a Hamish-man."

"Be he thin or be he thick," chanted Thomas, "he's eaten so much cake he's gonna be sick."

Hamish, who was certainly looking rather green, glared at them.

3. *On the Carpet*

As part of their project on mountains, Mr Majeika was taking Class Three to a museum where they could see some of the things from the famous expedition to climb Mount Everest.

"What a bore," said Hamish Bigmore.

The day of the outing started badly. It was pouring with rain, and the bus that was to take Class Three was late in arriving at St Barty's. Mr Potter was cross with the driver for keeping everyone waiting, and the driver was even crosser with Mr Potter, because he said he had been given the name of the wrong school, and it was Mr Potter's fault.

At last they were all on board, and Mr Potter waved goodbye to them all. But no

sooner had they driven away from St Barty's than Melanie started to cry and said she was feeling sick. Mr Majeika asked the driver to stop the bus, and Melanie got out. But she wasn't sick, she just got soaked with rain. She got back on the bus, and off they all went again.

This happened twice more, until at last Mr Majeika told her they couldn't go on stopping, and she would just have to put up with feeling sick until they got to the museum. This just made Melanie cry louder.

Then it was discovered that Hamish Bigmore, who was sitting at the back, had been eating his way through the nicest things in all the packed lunches, which were in a big box next to his seat. Mr Majeika told him to go up to the front and stay there. But this was worse, because Hamish began to annoy the driver.

First he said he wanted the radio on. When the driver had switched it on, Hamish told him to turn it off again because the music was boring. Next he said he wanted the cold air switched on, and then the hot air. Then he told the driver that they weren't going the quickest way to the town where the museum was. And then he started to give him instructions on how to drive the bus.

"You can overtake that car now, it's not going very fast. You ought to change into a lower gear, then you could get up this hill quicker. And start your windscreen-wipers, it's raining again. Watch out! You nearly hit that bike."

After a bit of this, the driver stopped the bus and said that either Hamish Bigmore got out and walked the rest of the way, or he wouldn't drive another inch. Mr Majeika finally persuaded him to agree to go on if Hamish Bigmore sat in the middle of the bus, some distance from the driver, but not near the packed lunches.

But even this wasn't much good, because Hamish started shouting things to the driver at the top of his voice. "Look out, driver, you nearly knocked an old lady down! Call yourself a driver? You couldn't even drive a lawnmower!"

So no one was very surprised when the driver announced on reaching the museum: "If you think I'm going to take you lot back this evening, you're very much mistaken." With this, he drove off.

"Oh dear," said Mr Majeika. "But I'm sure he didn't mean it. Come on, let's go into the museum."

And off they went, and they had a very good day, except that Hamish broke into a glass-case containing a bar of chocolate that had been taken to the top of Everest, and ate some of it before the attendant could stop him. Mr Majeika had difficulty persuading the museum people not to call the police. "Can't think why they're making all that fuss," said Hamish. "The rotten old chocolate was stale anyway."

When they came out of the museum it was still raining, and there was no sign of the bus. They waited for half an hour, but no bus turned up. "Oh dear," said Mr Majeika, "I'm afraid the driver meant what he said."

"Couldn't you telephone the bus company," said Jody, "and ask them to send another bus?" Mr Majeika went to use the telephone in the museum, but it had closed, and none of the phone boxes in the area was working.

"This is dreadful," said Mr Majeika. "What are we going to do?" Melanie began to cry.

"Why don't you take us back by magic?" said Pete.

"I'd love to," said Mr Majeika. "But I don't know any spells that would take a whole classful of children on a fifty-mile journey."

"I know," said Jody. "A magic carpet. That would do it."

Mr Majeika smiled. "Yes, I suppose it would, if I happened to have one here, and it was big enough. But my own magic carpet is tucked away in a cupboard at home, and, anyway, it's far too small."

"What makes a carpet into a magic carpet?" asked Thomas.

"Just spells," said Mr Majeika. "But rather a lot of them."

"So any carpet would do?" said Jody.

"I suppose so," said Mr Majeika, "if you had the time and the patience to say all the spells."

"There's a huge carpet in the entrance hall of the museum," said Jody. "A lovely, big Eastern carpet with fantastic patterns of animals and snakes and magical beasts. And it's quite big enough for us all to sit on."

Mr Majeika smiled. "It sounds just the thing," he said. "But the museum is locked up now, and, anyway, after all the trouble Hamish caused, they wouldn't take kindly to my borrowing their carpet."

"Surely," said Pete, "you know some

spells to open locked doors, Mr Majeika?"

Mr Majeika thought for a moment. "Well, yes, I do, but they'd have burglar alarms that would go off, and, besides, it would be stealing."

"You could get the carpet out in a minute or two," said Jody, "and you could bring it back tomorrow. Oh, *do* try, Mr Majeika."

Mr Majeika looked worried. "It'll take more than a minute to say all the spells," he said. Then his face brightened. "I've got it!" he said. "I can say the spells while the door is still locked, so that by the time we go in there, the carpet will already be magic, and I'll only have to give the command and it will rise into the air. And I suppose you're right about it not being stealing. Anyway, a proper magic carpet always returns to the place it's come from. You just have to give it the command

'Home!' and off it goes.''

"Hurray," said Thomas. "That's all easy then. Come on, Mr Majeika, what are we waiting for?"

Looking rather nervous, Mr Majeika assembled all Class Three on the museum steps, then shut his eyes, muttered lots of words and waved his hands at the museum doors. The doors began to shake, and then suddenly sprang open.

Everyone cheered – but then a bell began to ring. "The burglar alarm!" gasped Mr Majeika. "Quick, or the police will catch us. Hurry, hurry!"

Everyone ran in through the doors and sat down on the carpet. "This is stupid," grumbled Hamish. "Whoever heard of a flying carpet? Oooops!" He fell on his back as the carpet, under Mr Majeika's instructions, began to rise swiftly into the air.

"Three cheers for Mr Majeika!" shouted Thomas. "We'll be back at school in no time!"

"We'll be *somewhere* in no time," said Pete, "but it may be prison. Look!" With its blue light flashing and siren wailing, a large police car was drawing up outside the museum.

"Quick!" called Mr Majeika to the carpet. "Fast as you can! Take us home!"

The carpet zoomed out of the museum door and over the heads of the astonished policemen.

"Blimey, sarge," said one of them, "did you see what I saw, or was there something funny in that tea we've been drinking?"

The carpet was high above the museum now, whizzing through the pouring rain. Melanie said she was feeling carpet-sick and started to cry, but everyone else was loving it.

After a few minutes, Jody said: "Mr Majeika, isn't that the sea down there?"

Mr Majeika peered over the edge of the carpet. "Yes, Jody," he said. "We're going very fast, it shouldn't be long now."

"But we oughtn't to be crossing the sea to get to St Barty's," said Jody. "The carpet is going in the wrong direction."

"Oh dear," said Mr Majeika, "I must have given it the wrong instructions. Now, what did I say?"

"You said 'Take us home'," said Pete.

"How very silly of me," said Mr Majeika. "The carpet is taking us to *its* home – across the sea, to the Eastern land where it was made."

"That sounds much more fun than St Barty's," said Jody.

"Yes," said Mr Majeika, "but Mr Potter

and your mums and dads won't be very pleased if you land up somewhere in the Far East, and they have to come and fetch you. I must give the carpet some more instructions." He cleared his throat. "I'm frightfully sorry," he said to the carpet, "but this isn't quite what I wanted. Could you please take me to *my* home?"

The carpet stopped in mid-air, then zoomed off – upwards. It was like being in a very fast lift. Everyone said "Oooooo!" and clutched their stomachs, and Melanie cried even more. Even Mr Majeika looked pale.

"What's it doing?" shouted Thomas over the noise of rushing air. "Why are we going up into the sky?"

Mr Majeika slapped himself on his forehead. "I'm an idiot," he said. "It's not taking us to St Barty's, but to my *real* home, the land in the sky where the wizards come from. This is dreadful! All the other wizards are going to be very cross if I suddenly arrive with a party of schoolchildren. Stop!" he shouted to the carpet. The carpet stopped.

"I must describe St Barty's," said Mr Majeika. "Then the carpet will know where I mean." He thought for a moment, then he said: "Please would you take us to a big building surrounded by a high wall with railings?" The carpet immediately started to move.

"Are you sure you've told it enough, Mr Majeika?" asked Jody. "There are a lot of buildings that look like that."

"Oh dear, I suppose there are," said Mr Majeika. "But it's not easy to say what the school looks like. Ah, we're arriving now."

They were indeed arriving, but not at St Barty's. They had landed on the lawn of a big building surrounded by iron railings –

a very big building.

"This looks familiar," said Thomas. "I'm sure I've seen it somewhere before."

"And what do you think you're doing?" said a voice. It was a lady in a coat, with a scarf over her head, and two dogs on leads.

"Are we anywhere near St Barty's?" asked Mr Majeika.

"Certainly not," said the woman. "Now, be off with you, before I call my guards."

"Get us out of here, please," said Mr Majeika to the carpet, which obediently took off again. "I wonder who she was," he said, when they were well clear of the garden.

"Didn't you recognize her, Mr Majeika?" asked Jody. "It was the Queen."

"Oh dear," sighed Mr Majeika, "this is proving a bothersome business. I'll have to try again. Now listen," he said to the carpet, "we need to get back to *school*, do you understand?" The carpet gave a sort of shake, which seemed to mean "Yes", and off they went again.

"The Queen didn't seem surprised to see a magic carpet," said Thomas.

"I expect she's got one of her own," said Mr Majeika. "In the old days, kings and queens always had magic carpets, though they kept fairly quiet about it. Ah, this looks more hopeful – I think the carpet is taking us to the right place this time."

Certainly they were landing somewhere that looked much more like St Barty's. But it wasn't quite the same. The school buildings looked very grim, and in the playground some children in very old-fashioned clothes were being marched up and down by a fierce-looking woman with a cane.

"Classes One and Two!" she was shouting. "Indoors at once and eat up your gruel. This afternoon you have to learn the names and dates of all the kings and queens of England, and anyone who makes a mistake in the test will be given a taste of *this*. Class Three! Where is Class Three?"

"Er, here," said Mr Majeika nervously.

"Ssh, Mr Majeika," said Jody, "she doesn't mean us. Can the carpet take us for journeys in time as well as distance?"

"Oh, certainly," said Mr Majeika. "But you don't think–?"

"That explains it," said Jody. "We're back in Victorian times. This is what St Barty's used to be like."

The woman marched up to Class Three. "On your feet when I'm speaking to you!" she roared. "And who is this person?" She pointed at Mr Majeika.

"It's our teacher, Mr Majeika," said Thomas.

"Teacher? This isn't Class Three's teacher," snapped the woman. "Class Three is taken by Miss Barebones. Ah, here she comes now." And an even fiercer woman, also carrying a cane under her arm, began to march out of the school building.

"Quick!" said Mr Majeika to the carpet. "Get us out of this!" The carpet rose in the air, and though the two teachers shouted and waved their canes, it had taken off before they could grab hold of it. "Now," said Mr Majeika anxiously, "please take us forwards in time again."

Everything went very black and whirry, and Class Three shut their eyes. When they opened them, they saw that the carpet was again landing in a school playground. At least, they could recognize it as a playground, because there was a climbing-frame and a netball post. But everything else looked very different.

The school buildings were modern and shiny, and everywhere there were lights flashing on and off, and strange beeping sounds. A big digital noticeboard said:

ST BARTY'S HI-TECH SCHOOL
Date: 5 February 2091   Time: 16.48
Tomorrow's timetable:
The St Barty's Astronauts will be racing St James's Astronauts to the planet Mars. Class Three will go on an expedition to the Antarctic, in the school mini-nuclear-submarine. Dinner menu: nutrition capsules and recycled water.

"Goodness," said Mr Majeika. "I think we've gone rather too far forward in time."

"Give your names and identification numbers," said a mechanical voice. A

robot was walking towards them from one
of the school buildings, its eyes flashing
and strange whirring noises coming from
its head. Under its arm it carried a large
spanner.

"I think that's the head teacher," said
Jody. "And I don't like the look of that
spanner – if we're not careful, we'll be
dismantled. I don't think things look much
nicer in the future than in Victorian times."

"Come on, Mr Majeika," said Thomas.

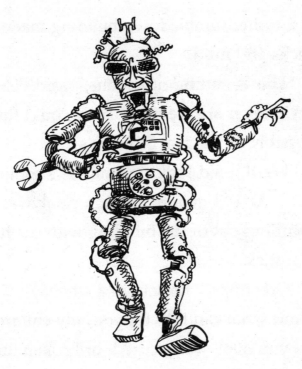

"Do your best to get us back to the real St Barty's."

"I'll try to," said Mr Majeika anxiously. "Carpet! Please take us to the real St Barty's!"

Everything went black again, and the carpet whizzed them round and round. When it came to a halt, they saw they were in the middle of open countryside, in front of a rather tumbledown building made of sticks and mud.

"This is getting ridiculous," said Pete. "Wherever are we now? How could this possibly be the real St Barty's?"

"Wait!" said Jody. "Someone's coming out." An old man in a rough cloak was shuffling out of the building with the help of a stick.

"Greetings," he said in a wheezy voice. "And what can I do for you, my children? Do you need warts cured, or broken limbs mended, or witches' curses removed? Just tell me, and I'll do my best."

"Who on earth is he?" whispered Thomas.

"He looks rather like a wizard," whispered Mr Majeika. Aloud, he said to the old man: "Excuse me, sir, but what is your name?"

"Bartholomew," answered the old man.

"Though some people call me Barty."

"Not Saint Barty?" asked Jody breathlessly.

The old man smiled. "I'm no saint," he said. "But folk round here do call me that when I've worked cures for them, or done some other little thing."

"We come from hundreds of years in the future," said Thomas, "and our school is named after you."

The old man scratched his head. "Who'd have thought it?" he said, smiling. "So you're from a distant time, are you? Best be getting back there, I reckon."

"We'd love to," said Mr Majeika. "But every time I tell our magic carpet to take us there, we land up somewhere else. We want to get back to St Barty's School in the year 1991, but I just can't make the carpet understand."

"Let's see what a few quiet words will do," said the old man, and he bent over and muttered at the carpet, which quivered in reply. "Off you go now!" called the old man to Class Three, and the carpet lifted them up in the air. "Think of me, now and then!"

Everything went black, and they were whirred around as before. But this time when the carpet landed, they were back at school, and Mr Potter was coming out of the school building, looking anxiously at his watch.

"Ah, there you are, Majeika," he said. "I was getting worried about you. The bus company rang up to say that the bus had been delayed by a puncture, and when it reached the museum you weren't there. How did you get home?"

"By magic carpet," said Mr Majeika. "I mean, er, magically easily."

"We met St Barty, Mr Potter," said Jody.

"You don't say?" said Mr Potter vaguely, disappearing towards his office.

"That old man really must have been a wizard," said Mr Majeika, "to get the carpet to bring us back here. I wonder what he said to it?"

"I heard him," said Hamish Bigmore. "He said, 'Take them back to St Barty's School in the year 1991.'"

"It's quite true, Mr Majeika," said Pete, who had overheard the old man too. "You kept trying to think of clever ways to instruct the carpet, but you never told it plainly."

Mr Majeika sighed. "Oh dear," he said, "I really am quite useless as a wizard. I think I'd better stick to teaching."

"You weren't useless at all, Mr Majeika," said Jody. "You gave us the best school expedition we've ever had!"

Also in Young Puffin

Mr Majeika

and the
Haunted Hotel

Humphrey Carpenter

Spooks and spectres at the *Green Banana*!

Class Three of St Barty's are off on an outing to
Hadrian's Wall with their teacher, Mr Majeika (who
happens to be a magician). Stranded in the fog when the
tyres of their coach are mysteriously punctured, they
take refuge in a nearby hotel called the Green Banana.
Soon some very spooky things start to happen. Strange
lights, ghostly sounds and vanishing people . . .

Also in Young Puffin

Mr Majeika

and the
School Book Week

Humphrey Carpenter

"Gosh," said Thomas, "isn't that Robin Hood?"

When St Barty's School have their Book Week, you can
be sure that Mr Majeika brings the characters alive – but
how can he make them go back into their books? And
when a new PE teacher organizes an Olympic Sports
Day and has Hamish Bigmore winning every event –
there has to be magic in the air! This is not going to be
an ordinary week . . .

Also in Young Puffin

Mr Majeika

and the
Music Teacher

Humphrey Carpenter

"Music teacher? What music teacher? I don't know anything about any music teacher."

It's a new term at St Barty's and the school is in uproar. Awful noises come from Class Three, angry parents fill the school and poor Mr Majeika is really frightened. Why? A new music teacher is coming who plans to start a school orchestra, and as only Mr Majeika knows, Wilhelmina Worlock is a witch!

Mr Majeika

and the
School Inspector

Humphrey Carpenter

"Use of magic by teacher strictly forbidden."

Poor Mr Majeika gains so many penalty points when
the nasty Mr Postlethwaite, a school inspector, comes to
inspect St Barty's School that he very nearly loses his
teacher's licence. However, at Barty Castle Mr Majeika
gets his revenge when he arranges for the inspector to
have a very chilling encounter!

Read more in Puffin

For complete information about books available from Puffin – and Penguin – and how to order them, contact us at the appropriate address below. Please note that for copyright reasons the selection of books varies from country to country.

www.puffin.co.uk

In the United Kingdom: Please write to Dept EP, Penguin Books Ltd,
Bath Road, Harmondsworth, West Drayton, Middlesex UB7 0DA

In the United States: Please write to Penguin Group (USA), Inc., P.O. Box 12289,
Dept B, Newark, New Jersey 07101–5289 or call 1–800–788–6262

In Canada: Please write to Penguin Books Canada Ltd,
10 Alcorn Avenue, Suite 300, Toronto, Ontario M4V 3B2

In Australia: Please write to Penguin Books Australia Ltd,
250 Camberwell Road, Camberwell, Victoria 3124

In New Zealand: Please write to Penguin Books (NZ) Ltd,
Private Bag 102902, North Shore Mail Centre, Auckland 10

In India: Please write to Penguin Books India Pvt Ltd,
11 Panscheel Shopping Centre, Panscheel Park, New Delhi 110 017

In the Netherlands: Please write to Penguin Books Netherlands bv,
Postbus 3507, NL–1001 AH Amsterdam

In Germany: Please write to Penguin Books Deutschland GmbH,
Metzlerstrasse 26, 60594 Frankfurt am Main

In Spain: Please write to Penguin Books S. A., Bravo Murillo 19,
1° B, 28015 Madrid

In Italy: Please write to Penguin Italia s.r.l.,
Via Felice Casati 20, I–20124 Milano

In France: Please write to Penguin France S. A.,
17 rue Lejeune, F–31000 Toulouse

In Japan: Please write to Penguin Books Japan, Ishikiribashi Building,
2–5–4, Suido, Bunkyo-ku, Tokyo 112

In South Africa: Please write to Longman Penguin Southern Africa (Pty) Ltd,
Private Bag X08, Bertsham 2013